Nathan Levy's

STORIES WITH HOLES
VOLUME 20

A collection of original thinking activities for improving inquiry!

An N.L. Associates, Inc. book

N.L. Associates, Inc.
PO Box 1199
Hightstown, NJ 08520

Library of Congress Catalog Number 89-92195
ISBN 1-878347-46-2

Printed in the United State of America

i

PREFACE – by Nathan Levy

This book is the result of several years' accumulation of ideas leading to puzzling stories that lend themselves to what I call thinking games. The "games" have become the means for thousands of people to carry on a totally enjoyable process of engaging critical and imaginative thinking. Volume 1 of my Stories with Holes is a collection of stories that has been gathered from various sources. Nathan Levy's Stories with Holes Volumes 2-20 are original. Wherever I speak I share some of the stories with my training groups. Teachers, parents and children enjoy the stories immensely. I hope you will as well.

INTRODUCTION

The objectives of using <u>Nathan Levy's Stories with Holes</u> include the following:

- to provide for growth in imagination and intuitive functioning
- to give experiences that display the fun of working cooperatively, rather than competitively, on a common problem
- to increase cognitive skills of resolving discrepancies through successful experiences
- to provide enjoyable changes-of-pace for task-oriented learning environments

This is a structured activity. It is designed to ensure involvement on the part of each participant, and to promote feelings of group and individual success.

The games are designed to accommodate all levels. "Children" from ages 8-88 will benefit from using these stories.

The time a story takes will vary. Usually a story lasts from 3 to 20 minutes, but some stories can take hours. Teachers often open or close a class period with a story or use one whenever a change of pace is required.

Children, lower grades through high school, tend to regard these thinking games as play instead of work. It is one of the few activities I know of that "hooks" almost anyone into creative use of their intelligence, i.e. learning, almost in spite of themselves. Nathan Levy's Stories with Holes are for all groups – regardless of age, background or achievement level.

**Please note that I have revised the above introduction and the following methodology from the way they appeared in the original collection of Stories with Holes. The revisions are based on my current workshop experiences with children and adults.

N.L.

iv

METHODOLOGY

The first time a group plays, it will be necessary to begin by announcing something like the following: "I am going to tell you a story with a hole in it – I mean that an important part of the story is missing. Listen carefully so you can find the missing part, for the story may not seem to make much sense to you at first..."

At this point, tell the story once, pause, and then tell it the same way again. Then say...

"You can ask questions that can be answered either with a "yes" or with a "no". I can only answer "yes", "no", "does not compute", or "is not relevant". If I answer, "does not compute", that means that the question you asked cannot receive a straight "yes" or "no" without throwing you off the track."

Allow for questions about the process, if there are any, but usually it is best simply to jump into the game by having the questioning start. The process becomes clear as the game progresses. Once a group has played the game, the full directions given above for playing the game are unnecessary.

From this point on, answer only in one of the four designated ways. The following is an example of a computed story taken from Stories with Holes, and how it might be played:

v

Story: David lives on the twentieth floor of an apartment building. Every time he leaves, he rides a self-service elevator from the twentieth floor to the street; but every time he returns, he rides the same self-service elevator only to the fifteenth floor, where he leaves the elevator and walks up the remaining five flights of stairs. Repeat, then ask who knows the answer already; if any do, ask them to observe and not give away the answer.

Question: Does the elevator go all the way up?
Answer: Yes.
Q: Does he want the exercise?
A: No.
Q: Does it have something to do with the elevator not working right?
A: No.
Q: Does he have a girlfriend on the 15th floor who he stops to see?
A: No.
Q: Does he have something different about him?
A: Yes.
Q: Is he a robber?
A: No.
Q: Is he a real person?
A: Yes.
Q: A tall person?
A: No.
Q: Is his size important?
A: Yes.
Q: I know! He's too short to reach the button!
A: Right!

At this point, make certain that all the participants understand the answer and why it is the correct answer. In the example given above, the group found the answer quite soon. Instead of starting a new game -- particularly if this is the first time playing – spend some time processing the game with questions like:

* What did you have to do in order to play this game? (Listen, hear each answer, think, imagine, follow a line of reasoning, eliminate possibilities, etc.)

* Ask the person who finally solved the riddle, "Joanne, did you have help from others in finding the answer?" It nearly always comes out that the person relied on previous questions and answers. Use this to point out the interdependence of players, and reduce competition within the group to be the "winner".

* When do you see yourself having to use the kind of thinking you use in this game?

Usually a group of youngsters will be eager to try a second game right away. Generally, it is best to wait, and string the games out as a series over several weeks or months. The only time it might be advisable to do a second game right away is when the story is somehow solved in a minute or less – too soon for the group to "get into it".

Some important points to remember:

1. Immediately following the telling of each story and before the questioning begins, ask if anyone in the group has heard it before and knows the answer. Tell these people to observe and refrain from questioning.

2. Use the "does not compute" response whenever a single word or phrase in a question makes it impossible to answer with a "yes" or "no" answer. Examples from the story above:

   - "Why does he live on the twentieth floor?" "Why" questions, as well as "where, who, when or which", cannot be answered "yes" or "no".

   - "Does the elevator operator make him get off at the fifteenth floor?" No mention was made of an operator.

3. If a game goes past 10 or 12 minutes and some people begin to lose interest, close the game for the present. There is absolutely nothing harmful in leaving the puzzle unsolved. The group can return to it another time, when interest and energy are high. Some students may protest, but do not give the answer. The experience of non-closure provides some valuable learning in itself; but more importantly, once a group has expended considerable energy on the game, the victory should be an earned one. Although there may be some unusual circumstances under which you would give the group the answer, I have found it best not to do so (even if some are begging). The point here is not to "take the answer

viii

away by giving it." You can always return to it later. What is important is that the students earn the feeling of "we-did-it!"

4. Share the computer (leader) role. Once kids have learned how the game works, have a volunteer lead the game. He or she can choose from the stories in this book and read the answer. As soon as you are convinced the student is familiar with the story, the answer, and the process (which you should previously have modeled) have the leader read the story to the class, change into the helpful computer, and begin taking questions. Be sure to pass the leadership role around, for many will wish to take part. Most important here is what you model. A child-led story is an excellent small-group activity to have going on while you are occupied elsewhere in the classroom.

5. Encourage categorical thinking. When a player asks a question beginning, "Would it help us to know..." or "Does it have anything to do with..." pause in the game and show how the type of question is uniquely helpful in narrowing down the range of questions, distilling and focusing the group's attention, or cutting away large slices of the topic that are irrelevant. Thus, the question "Is David's occupation important?" tends to be more useful than "Is he a plumber? A teacher", etc.

6. Be sure that a question is exactly true, or exactly false, before responding. One word can make the difference.

ix

1. Jennifer and Amy

Jennifer is in Missouri, Amy is in Oklahoma City, Emily is in Arkansas and Ellen is in Kansas. They all live in the same small one story house. How is this possible?

Answer:

They are not in the house together; they are all on separate vacations.

Contributed by Jeannie Bundy, LaCygne, KS.

2. Nicole and Rafael

The son shining in St. Louis made the lives of Nicole and Rafael brighter in New Jersey.

Answer:

Nicole and Rafael were an older married couple whose son owned a prosperous shoe shining business at the St. Louis airport. He sent money for their care because his business did so well.

3. Rain

This year April Showers brought May flowers in snowy December.

A **nswer:**

April Showers is a girl who brought May (her friend) flowers in December.

Contributed by Nathan Jokela and Anthony Ays, Naples, FL.

3

4. The Drummers

The drummers drummed, the horns played, the fiddlers fiddled, the marchers marched, yet the parade was a dismal failure on this beautifully sunny July 4th day.

A nswer:

Two of the "fiddlers" were the bus drivers who "fiddled around" too long and arrived too late to get to the parade on time. As they waited, the band members warmed up (played) and the marchers loosened up (marched), but they never got the chance to get to the parade, which was a dull affair without the band.

5. Michie the Heroine

"Rose Michie stopped the man's laughter. She is a true heroine and should be rewarded handsomely," said the local newspaper.

The paper's misuse of space misled many people.

Answer:

The paper wrote "man's laughter," when it meant to write "manslaughter." Rose Michie had saved the life of several people with her quick thinking and bravery.

6. What Camille Said

Camille said, "I is."

Antoine said, "I is not!"

Camille spoke perfectly correctly.

Antoine did not.

Answer:

Camille was answering the question, "What is the ninth letter of the alphabet?"

7. Cat Conspiracy

"I'm telling you, that author is out to hurt cats."

"Why do you think that?"

"I can tell by his writings."

"Now that you say that, I agree. That mouse lover!"

Answer:

They are lamenting that Nathan Levy keeps creating holes for mice to hide in when he writes his <u>Stories with Holes</u> books.

Note: This story should only be used by pupils who are familiar with <u>Nathan Levy's Stories with Holes</u>.

8. The Two Brothers

Two brothers were playing on their front lawn. There was a street in front of their house. Across the street, there was a park. In the park were two men, a woman and three children. The brothers decided to go into their house for a while. They watched their favorite TV show and had some hot chocolate. A few hours later they went back out to play on their front lawn. When they looked over into the park, one of the men, the woman and the three children were still there. The other man had not left the park – but he was no longer there!

Answer:

He was a snowman and the sun had melted him.

This story was written by Glynnis Baker, a student in the Selinsgrove Area School District, Selinsgrove, PA.

9. It Is

When he is on it, it is. When he is not on it, it is not. Who is he and what is it?

Answer:

It is Air Force One. When the President is on it, It is called Air Force One.

Contributed by Marci Nichols, Batavia, OH.

10. Ms. Latif, the Visitor

The faculty members of Appletree Middle School all explained to the principal that Ms. Latif, a visiting speaker, said her Brown Cabinet spoke to her. At first no one believed her, but after thinking about it they were convinced she was not lying.

Answer:

Ms. Latif was the President of a large corporation. Her cabinet was the Secretary, Treasurer, etc. The Chairman of the Board was Mr. Arnold Brown. Therefore, she called them her "Brown Cabinet".

This story idea was contributed by Sarah Latif from Overland Park, KS.

11. Ted – The Swift

Ted's healthy diet of fresh fish and meat has made him the fastest mountain climber in the world. Even though Ted is now old, bald and toothless no man or woman can come close to matching Ted's speed.

Answer:

Ted is a bald eagle.

This story idea was contributed by Ben Neufeld, from Overland Park, KS.

12. Paige & Jennifer's Time Travel

Paige and Jennifer were sent back to the time before fire was invented. With them they carried fire sticks. Their fire sticks could not burn or heat anything, but they were very useful. Matches would also be taken on the next trip back to this time in history.

Answer:

The "fire sticks" were flashlights needed to help Paige and Jennifer see in the dark.

This story idea was contributed by Paige and Jennifer Cain, students at Wynford Intermediate School, Bucyrus, Ohio.

13. Andrea's Trip Across Arizona

Andrea was climbing in Arizona. She brought her dog Joe with her. She was on top of a mountain that had a 450 foot drop. Andrea stopped climbing and walked forward. Both Andrea and Joe made it across the mountain without incident.

Answer:

Andrea and Joe were in an airplane flying to Los Angeles.

This story idea was contributed by Erin Green.

14. Florida's Hurricane

Taryn Koslow, a native Floridian, experienced the worst hurricane in the history of the state of Florida, but was untouched. Every city (Miami, Ft. Lauderdale, Tallahassee, Naples, Tampa, etc.) was hit.

Answer:

Taryn watched the hurricane on TV in the state of Washington.

This story idea was contributed by Bryan Mayes, Jana Brooks, Justine Amos and Robyn Williams of Wakarusa, KS.

14

15. Baby Moe

Baby Moe was raised in a cavern as part of a large family. When she was six years old her mother took her out of the cavern. She was made comfortable for one night and then she disappeared and was never seen again. None of her relatives did anything to find Moe, even though it was very obvious Moe was missing.

Answer:

Baby Moe was a molar baby tooth. She fell out and was placed under little Jane's pillow. The tooth fairy took her away during the night.

Jane B. Moore of Arkdale, WI wrote this story.

15

16. No Way Out

Imagine you are in a haunted house. The doors are stuck, the windows are nailed shut. Attack dogs are right outside the doors and windows. All possible exits are blocked. Worst of all, you are tied to a chair with strong wire. You cannot get help. There is clearly a best way out!

Answer:

Stop imagining!

This story was contributed by Keith Torr, Tony Ballard, Russell Tarabour and Nick Tilipman from Livingston, NJ.

16

17. Mr. Hubbard and Ms. Yepez

After the conference, Mr. Hubbard, the parent of Kelly, called his child's teacher, Ms. Yepez, a jerk.

"Thank you", said Ms. Yepez.

Answer:

Mr. Hubbard, the parent, was a police officer who stopped the teacher, Ms. Yepez, for speeding. Since the police officer's child was in the teacher's class and he knew her well, he did not give Ms. Yepez a ticket. However, the police officer said, "Don't be a jerk when you drive down this street. You were going too fast."

18. Dominique the Magician

Dominique the Magician was busy on this snowy winter day. She was trying to create a huge snowman that could actually move. Dominique succeeded. Later that day she showed the moving snowman to an audience. The audience was not the least bit surprised.

Answer:

Dominique created a hand puppet snowman.

Thanks to David Roberts of Ruby Thomas Elementary School, Las Vegas, NV.

18

19. The Train Conductor

The Train conductor got The Train moving. In almost record time, The Train went from New York to San Francisco. The conductor stopped only briefly as he drove The Train on this eventful trip. Not one mile registered on the odometer.

Answer:

The Train was the name of an orchestra. First they played "New York, New York" and then they played, "I Left My Heart in San Francisco".

20. Tony's Bar Visit

Tony walked into the bar. He did not have a drink, he fought with no one, but he left with a bloody nose. The next day he walked into a different bar, had a strong drink, got into two arguments, but came out without injury.

Answer:

The first time he walked into a metal bar and hit his nose.

This story idea was contributed by Keith Torr, Tony Ballard, Russell Tarabour and Nick Tilipman of Livingston, NJ.

20

ABOUT THE AUTHOR

Nathan Levy

Nathan Levy is the author of more than 40 books which have sold almost 250,000 copies to teachers and parents in the US, Europe, Asia, South America, Australia and Africa. His unique Stories with Holes series continues to be proclaimed the most popular activity used in gifted, special education and regular classrooms by hundreds of educators. An extremely popular, dynamic speaker on thinking, writing and differentiation, Nathan is in high demand as a workshop leader in school and business settings. As a former school principal, company president, parent of four daughters and management trainer, Nathan's ability to transfer knowledge and strategies to audiences through humorous, thought provoking stories assures that participants leave with a plethora of new ways to approach their future endeavors.

For more information about Mr. Levy's books and workshops please call 732-605-1643, write to N.L. Associates, PO Box 1199, Hightstown, NJ 08520, email him at nlevy103@comcast.net or visit his website at www.storieswithholes.com.

NL Associates is pleased to be the publisher of this book. Teachers, students and other readers are invited to contribute their own "Stories with Holes" for possible inclusion in future volumes. Suggested stories will not be returned to you and will be acknowledged only if selected. Please send your suggestions to:

NL Associates Inc
PO Box 1199
Hightstown NJ 08520

Dynamic Speakers
Creative Workshops
Relevant Topics

Nathan Levy, author of the <u>Stories with Holes</u> series and <u>There Are Those</u>, and other nationally known authors and speakers, can help your school or organization achieve positive results with children. We can work with you to provide a complete in-service package or have one of our presenters lead one of several informative and entertaining workshops.

Workshop Topics Include:
- Practical Activities for Teaching Gifted Children
- Critical Thinking Skills
- Teaching Gifted Children in the Regular Classroom
- How to Read, Write and Think Better
- Using <u>Stories with Holes</u> and Other Thinking Activities
- Powerful Strategies to Enhance the Learning of Your Gifted and Highly Capable Students
- Powerful Strategies to Help Your Students With Special Needs be More Successful Learners
- The Principal as an Educational Leader
and many more…